God made you BEAUTIFUL

DEDICATED TO ALL THE LITTLE GIRLS IN THE WORLD!

GOD MADE YOU BEAUTIFUL
A BEDTIME STORY
BY K.S. HORNE

DISCOVER MORE STORIES
AT KSHORNE.COM

WHEN GOD MADE THE TREES
THE BIRDS AND THE BEES

THE OCEAN WITH WAVES THE WIND AND THE BREEZE

GOD MADE YOU BEAUTIFUL
JUST LIKE ALL OF THESE

HE THOUGHT OF THE THINGS
THAT HE LOVED THE MOST

AND MADE YOU MY LITTLE GIR
NOT TRYING TO BOAST

He said Let's make eyes
A chocolatey brown

THAT SWEET IS MY
FAVORITEST CANDY
around

OD PULLED SOME FROM HEAVEN AND SOME THINGS FROM EARTH

AND SAID SHE'LL BE PERFECT
FOR ALL THAT IT'S WORTH

GOD SAID LET'S MAKE HAIR
LIKE THE WOOL OF THE LAMB

SO I CAN SEE FROM WAY UP HERE
THAT SHE'S PART OF MY FAM

OH LET'S MAKE HER MIND AS STRONG AS THE OCEAN

SO THAT WHEN SOMETHING'S
NOT RIGHT
SHE WILL CAUSE A COMMOTION

AND GIVE HeR A WILL THAT WIL
BenD AND NOT BReAK

he WOrLD DEFINITELY NEEDS THAT
or GOODNESS SAKE

he said let's make some skin
ooohh brown will be fun
so that she can spend hours
outside in the sun

OH AND LET'S NOT FORGET
HER MOST BEAUTIFUL NOSE
SO THAT SHE CAN SMELL EVERY
FLOWER AND ROSE

AND WHEN HE WAS DONE
HE GAVE YOU HIS SMILE
SO BRIGHT YOU BRING JOY
FROM AS FAR AS A MILE

"IT IS FINISHED" HE SAID
AS HE SENT YOU TO ME
SO STRONG AND SO BEAUTIFU
LOVING AND FREE

Made in the USA
Middletown, DE
16 December 2022

18842316R20024

R.S. Horne believes that all of God's children are beautiful, and that they should be reminded of it every day!

These books are created to fill every child who reads them with feelings of confidence and love.Know that you are blessed by God, and remember that you are His beautiful creation.

See you in the next book! Let's build stronger children together!

ISBN 9798649077309